A Centennial Publication
of the
Hebrew Union College
Jewish Institute of Religion

A SONG
TO
CREATION

A Dialogue with a Text

by

EUGENE MIHALY

Cincinnati
Hebrew Union College Press
1975

To Cecile

who taught me the melody

Table of Contents

I

AN ONGOING
REVELATION

I

AN ONGOING REVELATION

R. Aḥa said, "Matters which were not revealed to Moses were revealed to R. Akiba and his colleagues."
—Pesikta Kahana IV, *Parah*

When Moses ascended on high (to receive the Torah), he found the Holy One, blessed be He, knotting crowns to the letters.
(A number of letters in the Scroll of the Pentateuch are written with three small strokes in the form of a crown, taggin, *placed on top.)*

Moses said to His Presence, "Master of the Universe, who restrains your hand?"
(The "crowns" intimate the deeper meanings implicit in the written Torah, and Moses asked why God did not reveal them to him.)

God replied, "There is a man who will appear after many generations by the name of Akiba, son of

Joseph, and he will infer from every jot and tittle mounds upon mounds of laws."

(Not until many centuries after Moses will the myriad of laws and customs hidden in the words and markings of the written Torah be revealed, through the brilliant and intricate exegesis of Akiba.)

Moses said to His Presence, "Master of the Universe, show him to me."

God said, "Turn around!"
(The past is known, "visible," and is, therefore, considered to be in front of man; the future, hidden from sight, is in back of him. Moses had to turn around to see the future.)

Moses turned around. He went and sat at the end of eighteen rows (in the academy of R. Akiba).
(Moses humbly seated himself in the last row of the academy. He listened intently to the discussion, but it was incomprehensible to him.)

He did not know what they were saying and his strength failed him.

When Akiba arrived at a particular conclusion, his disciples said to him, "Whence do you know this?"

Akiba said to them, "It is a law given to Moses at Sinai."

When Moses heard this, he was immediately mollified.

Moses returned to the presence of the Holy One, blessed be He. He said to His Presence, "Master of the Universe, you have a man like this and you give the Torah through me!"

God said to him, "Be silent! Thus have I decided."

—Menaḥot 29b and Yalkut Shimoni I.173

II

A LIVING
TORAH

II

A LIVING TORAH

The teacher of Torah in a liberal Jewish seminary shares much with the academician, the teacher of humanities in the graduate school of a university. But he has his own genius. Perhaps the uniqueness of his teaching may be best described by the expression, *Torat Ḥayyim*—a living Torah: not a literature alone, but also a here-and-now experience.

Torah emerges dialectically, not as a series of suspended, theoretical absolutes which may be recorded for all times, but as an ongoing dialogue within the religious consciousness of a community—a dialogue between a past and a future, the moorings and the reach. A biblical verse viewed as Torah encompasses the totality; it is timeless and ever timely; past, future, and present merge in the reality of the now. This is the uniqueness of Torah; it overcomes time.

As Torah, the Exodus from Egypt, for example, is not a past event. It is paradigmatic—the model, the pattern for every act which makes man free. But it is more. To study the Egyptian Redemption as Torah is to dedicate, to worship, to adore. "Let my people go," calls now, here in the classroom. Pharaoh has a thousand familiar faces, and "my people" are every shade of black and white. But the Exodus is more still. As Torah, it is a redemptive experience, a realized eschatology *(me'ein 'olam haba)*. I am free and I know that "my Redeemer lives." I appropriate, I experience every redemptive moment of our total saga—the "was" and the "could be" are within my grasp. I feel the lash of the oppressor; I know the heart of the stranger, the outcast; I am in his place. And I perceive, too, the footsteps of man fulfilled, of a mankind reconciled *('Ikveta dim'shiḥa)*.

To read a biblical text as Torah is to listen—an involved, active listening. What did Moses hear, and what was his response? And then to listen on. What did Hillel hear as the verse addressed him in the first century B.C., and what was his answer? Yishmael carried on a dialogue with the verse, too, and Akiba built intricate structures on each jot of every letter. Ibn Ezra and Rashi and Naḥmanides, Luzzato and the Biurists, the Maskil and the Reformer of the nineteenth century, Geiger and Kohler and all the rest, on into our own day and beyond—our hopes and dreams, our farthest, most imaginative reach—they are all in a classic Jewish text when we study it prayerfully, as Torah.

The written word restrains, even as Torah; but it also roots. Moorings undeniably hold back; they inhibit; but they also anchor; they protect against caprice, against the temporary, the vogue, the superficial —against our substituting utopian irrelevancies for an authentic messianic reach. The text disciplines, but the Torah's urgent whisper, "Your fathers have set the precedent," urges and spurs us on to dare innovate and create Torah; to dare claim the true as it confronts and challenges us, and thus to find the *Torat Ḥayyim,* the doctrine of life, for ourselves and for those who shall follow.

The result has never been nor will it be a rigid uniformity. The range of responsible, authentic choice is very wide. But neither is the dedicated teacher, the creator of Torah, an isolated, groping "single one" lost in a miasma of subjectivity. Freedom—radical freedom—but within a context; the only possible freedom. No matter how much of the detail of classic Judaism we ultimately accept or reject, as long as we choose within the context of our historic continuum—as aware, conscious Jews—the essential will be present.

Every man is potentially *humanum*. That is one frame within which we make authentic choices. Some of us are Western man—and that provides yet another context for our freedom. On a deeper level—our finitude, our mortality, our passion for the infinite, *eros* and *thanatos,* our being subject and object, I–It and and I–Thou, *homo faber* and biologic man, or our being in a time-space continuum—all of these are attempts to define the human condition, the framework without which freedom is but delusion.

The crucial point for a teacher of Torah is that in addition to the conscious and unconscious, social and cultural elements of his frame, which he shares with others, he would exercise his freedom as a Jew. He would find and confront and transform himself and the world about him in an ongoing prayerful dialogue with Jeremiah, Joshua ben Ḥananyah, Saadyah Gaon and Krochmal, Shneur Zalman of Ladi and Samuel Hirsch and Franz Rosenzweig. His voice thus becomes the voice of Sinai—that ever-present Sinai—the source of every call rooted in a three-thousand-year reach and response. Classic rabbinic literature repeats four times: "Whatever a faithful, committed student will teach—whatever he will find in a text or say to it—Moses heard it at Sinai."

The goal of the modern teacher of Torah is study and worship—to confront and to appropriate; objective, scientific analysis—to be observer, and, at the same time, to enter the process and to direct it from within, to turn the wheel on which he is turning, to become part of the dialectic. His endeavor is to deepen commitment, to guide the student to appropriate the experience of his fathers so that he shall perceive, in the struggles of a Hillel or a Rabbi Tarphon, or in the dialogues of Judah Hanasi and Antoninus, the ground for his own being. The teacher's hope is that as the student immerses himself in his literary heritage, he will discover his own Jewish soul and perhaps distill from the tradition the imperatives and the dreams which constitute his own Jewishness.

And on occasion, after he has wrestled with the words and techniques, after he has tried to relive with his students the discourse and discussion of the ancient academy, the teacher feels a response—one of those rare and precious moments when the grasp overtakes the reach, when theoretical abstraction becomes a commandment, a *mitzvah*, a demand "thou shalt" and "thou shalt not," addressed to all, to each individual in the classroom—a demand so compelling and insistent that it elicits the response: "Yes! I must! I am a Jew! I can do no other!" And then student and teacher alike suddenly know that they are studying Torah—more, they are creating Torah.

Join me for an hour in the classroom, as we study and perhaps even pray a rabbinic text together. We shall consider a passage from Genesis Rabbah, the classic Midrash on the first book of the Bible.

III

THE TEACHER'S INTRODUCTION

III

THE TEACHER'S INTRODUCTION

In the beginning God created…Bereshit bara Elohim
—Genesis 1:1

Implicit in the midrashic exposition of a biblical text are a number of assumptions accepted without question by a second- or third-century audience, the context of the discourse—the thought patterns, canons of logic, literary forms, the psychology and the picture of reality current in the early centuries of the Christian Era. Just as we today communicate within a tacitly assumed context—when we use the word *earth*, for example, we do not feel it necessary to explain that we have in mind a sphere which revolves about the sun—so with the literary creativity of each age. Implicit in a text is the context, which must be made explicit if we are to recover the intent of the author or the meaning of a literary composition.

Man is, most often, unaware of significant aspects

of his environment. He accepts them unconsciously. He lives them. Just as we are normally oblivious of our heartbeat or of the air we breathe—the incessant cacophony all about us that we call silence—so are we largely unaware of the myths, the science, the cultural tools of our surroundings implicit in every word we utter. Only when the environment changes, when the heartbeat accelerates or falters, or perhaps during moments of heightened sensitivity, when we view ourselves and the world about us from the perspective of the poet or the artist, does the hidden become revealed and conscious.

The teacher in Lydda, Tiberias, or Caesaria during the classic rabbinic period could not, had he been so inclined, have specified many of the even obvious premises implied in his exposition of Scripture. And neither could the traditional Yeshiva student throughout the ages, despite his erudition and devotion. They did not have the necessary perspective. Many centuries would pass before a student could view the literature of the Rabbis from a new, postmedieval vantage point and thus come to appreciate the true meaning and significance of the contribution of the Rabbis.

When we today—with the aid of the techniques of literary criticism, a knowledge of history, and an awareness of the dynamics of human behavior—read a rabbinic text, we discern considerably more than the obvious literal meaning of the Hebrew or Aramaic words. As we approach a midrashic passage, we hear the Rabbi of the first or second or fifth century, regardless of the specific content of his discourse, open his lecture, in part, as follows:

The Bible, as we all know, is divinely revealed, Holy Writ. It is the source of all truth and all wisdom. If we know how to expound the Torah, if our deeds and motives are pure enough, and if we search deeply enough, the Bible provides a sure guide for all time and every circumstance.

Know, dear people, that nothing in Scripture is fortuitous or superfluous. Every letter, every jot, is there by design, carefully arranged by a Divine Intelligence to teach a significant lesson. There are numerous faces to the Torah. Each word is a seventy-faceted gem (the numerical value of yayin) *which sparkles a new and ever more brilliant ray as we turn it and turn it, again and again. The many levels of meaning are com-*

municated by way of hints, allusions, mnemonics, by means of intricate cipher codes, through metaphor and allegory.

The Torah addresses each man in accordance with his effort and capacity. But no mortal, bound by his finitude, can ever fathom the full depth of the Torah or even claim final authority for his interpretation of any one detail. A greater teacher may supersede him. The profundity of Scripture is never exhausted. Whatever a dedicated, inspired student derives from a biblical verse is present in the text—indeed, every conceivable insight was anticipated at Sinai, the ever-present Sinai, the sum of human possibility. The same holy spirit which permeates the Torah is potentially present in us and, if we are worthy, it will aid us in uncovering the truth imbedded in the words of Scripture.

The student in the ancient academy searched for truth in the most reliable source available to him, his sacred Scriptures. He utilized the finest tools at hand, the "scientific" methodology of his day—intricate hermeneutics, the subtle rules of exegesis formulated by the masters of his age: Hillel, Rabbi

Akiba, Rabbi Yishmael, Rabbi Eliezer, and Rabbi Meir. Every session was an adventure in discovery, a fascinating glimpse of ultimate reality. And, in addition, the student in the academy experienced the exaltation of prayer and adoration. He stood in God's presence—with all that such a stance implies; he was performing a *mitzvah;* he was doing God's will and fulfilling his own highest destiny.

Rabbinic literature will not teach us physics or cosmology, nor, in its literal form, even a viable system of ethics. The Rabbis, in most instances, will not even help us to understand the original meaning of the Bible—the literal intent of the biblical author who wrote within and out of his own environment, centuries before the rabbinic period. Rather than inferring his lesson from the Bible, the rabbinic "exegete" puts himself and his world into the words of Scripture. His exposition is mostly eisegesis, not exegesis. The scriptural text inspires him; it is his point of departure; but before the Rabbi is through gerrymandering, wrenching out of context, expurgating and "interpreting," the biblical text becomes largely a pretext.

But this literature, the vast labyrinth of the Talmud

and Midrash, if we study it on its own terms, seriously and in the light of its historic setting—without preconceived prejudice or value judgments—reveals to us the Jewish mind and soul in what is perhaps their most creative stage, certainly the stage most influential and crucial in the development of the faith of our fathers as well as our own.

Beyond the "tool-world" of the Rabbis—the antiquated political and social views and institutions, the archaic science—there emerges from this literature the essential Jewish ethos, that character and sentiment of the Jew, his unique spirit, which actuates his attitudes, practices, and ideals as he encounters and responds to changing circumstances. This ethos —the Jewish continuum—assumes the myriad guises of the environment in a state of constant change; it utilizes and manifests itself through the "tools-at-hand." This unique spirit, the Jewish continuum, is not independent of, and cannot be isolated from, the historic, concrete detail which gives the Jewish ethos flesh and substance.

But this continuum of the Jew never disappears. It never loses its essential identity. If our view is penetrating enough, we perceive an unbroken, continuous thread which leads us back to Hillel and Sinai and Abraham. It is this thread, the Jew's response to, and his transformation of, the environment, the permanent Torah—imbedded in a thousand concrete details, shrouded in countless transient myths, strengthened by strands added in every generation and discovered by our arduous probing of endless minutiae—it is this soul of the Jew that we would find and appropriate—and prayerfully apply—in our study of ancient rabbinic texts.

And now, to the specifics. The midrashic passage before us is in the nature of a comment on the opening chapter of Genesis, the very first verse in the Bible: "In the beginning God created...*Bereshit bara Elohim...*"

The time: The middle of the fourth century A.D.

The place: The academy in Tiberias on the shores of the Sea of Galilee.

IV

IN THE
ANCIENT ACADEMY

IV

IN THE ANCIENT ACADEMY

A. THE DISCOURSE

Note, dear students and colleagues," Rabbi Yonah opens his discourse, "that the first letter of our sacred Torah is a *B*, the letter *Bet* of *Bereshit*. One would reasonably expect that the Torah, the perfectly designed product of a Divine Intelligence, should begin with the first letter of the alphabet, the *Aleph*—and especially so since the subject is the beginning, creation. (Indeed, the ten commandments do open with the *Aleph: Anokhi Adonai Eloheikha*...) Why then does the creation story begin with the second letter, the *Bet*?

"It would seem that the *Bet* bids us pause and search more deeply, to uncover the profounder nuances hidden in the biblical text. For, surely, the Torah is more than a chronology or a theoretical explanation of remote origins. The primary intent of the Torah is to teach the way by which man shall live and not die. Well, let us, my fellow students and teachers, ponder this letter *Bet*—its shape, its numerical value, its order in the alphabet, the associations it evokes. Perhaps, with the help of the Merciful One, we shall succeed in discovering something of the wisdom that the infinite, omniscient Author of the Torah included in His account of the creation of the universe."

There is an intense stillness in the academy. The students are in deep thought—searching, praying: "What hidden mystery does this letter contain? Is it perhaps the key which will unlock the secrets of the deep and of the heavens—of the process of creation itself?"

The calm, gentle voice of Rabbi Yonah interrupts the reverie: "The question before us is not new. Our fathers considered the same problem. It is proper that we build on their conclusions. That is our blessing as Jews: We rarely need to begin *de novo;* we continue. Rabbi Levi, his memory is blessing, the great haggadist whom you hear me quote so often, suggested that the letter *Bet* was chosen because of its form. The shape of the Bet (ב)—closed on three sides, at the back, top, and bottom, and open only in front—defines the areas of man's competence, the domain which he shall explore with benefit to discover his vocation and thus fulfill his human potential.

"As one begins his study of the very first verse of the Bible," Rabbi Yonah elaborated, "the letter *Bet* says to him:

Face me, dear student, and become aware of your limitations and the rich possibilities. Let my shape define the range of your effective vision. That which is in back of me, the pre-creation, chaotic tohu-bohu or the secrets of cosmogony (ma'aseh bereshit), is beyond your ken. Nor shall you seek to scan that which is above me —the mysteries of the heavens and of the Chariot (ma'aseh merkhavah)—or that which is below me—the miasma of the deep, of the netherworld, under the Tehom. *All of these realms are closed to you. Even that which is in back of yourself as you face me—the end of days, the weird speculations on the apocalypse and the millennium —is hidden from your view. All that you can know, all that you need to know, is the created world—as it is—and the potential imbedded in it. The span from me to you, that which is before you, the phenomenal world and man's struggle within and with it, nature and history, the record of human experience—these are the proper focus for man's search and effort.*

"The sainted Bar Kapparah," continued Rabbi Yonah—"you recall that he was of the inner circle of Judah Hanasi, the one whose motto was 'Greater are the good deeds of righteous men than all the awesome wonders of the creation of heaven and earth'—derived the lesson which we find in the *Bet* from a verse in Deuteronomy (4:32): 'You have but to inquire about bygone ages that are before you, ever since God created man on earth (not before it) from one end of the horizon to the other (not above or below it): Has anything as grand as this ever happened or has its like ever been known?'

"Do you appreciate, dear colleagues," Rabbi Yonah stressed, "the full import of this message discovered in sacred Scripture by our fathers and bequeathed to us? It is a total view which is reflected in and directs the curriculum of the life of our people. The shape of the letter *Bet* tells us that we the bearers of this heritage, we of the congregation of Jacob, must not, cannot delude ourselves that we shall find the goals of human existence, our true destinies, by denigrating, by negating, the creaturely world. No simplistic, magical formula of 'ascent' or 'descent' will provide the answers."

Rabbi Yonah, now more urgent, exhorts his disciples: "Accept, embrace this created world as it is made known to you. The voice from Sinai, that insistent voice which we have internalized as a people, the Sinai within us, daily pleads, 'Do not dissipate your energy and your effort in an illusory escape from the inevitable tensions, the pain and ugliness and grandeur of the arduous creative process. Cosmos inheres in and emerges from the chaos of becoming. Face this human world; search, investigate, study it; find your role in it; work with it; improve and perfect it; the potential meaning and order are there for you to discover and actualize. That is your vocation as a people—your terrible, glorious destiny.'

"There are many in our land and beyond its borders—right there in Tiberias, as you well know, perhaps in our very midst," Rabbi Yonah continued, "who view all of creation, man and his natural drives and longings, even the most lofty and noble, as tainted, defiled—the product of an inferior deity, a petty craftsman, the corrupt creator, whom they call the 'demiurge.' They claim that the Creator, the one who fashioned this world, the God of history, is the 'revealed,' the 'known' god, an inferior deity. The miserable elements of this world, they say, the Creator's handiwork—the coercive laws which he has promulgated, the institutions which he has established—partake of his nature; they reflect the cosmic tyranny, the true essence of this petty, vindictive god of justice, of creation, and of law.

"In radical contrast to this revealed lawgiver, the 'just god,' the creator, the demiurge—the adherents of these groups, and they are legion, maintain—is the true, the good god—unknown, strange, alien to this world, wholly other. This transcendent god, the gracious and merciful one, the lord of love and compassion, stands in polar opposition to the created world. He is unknown in it and cannot be discovered through it. Only sparks of the hidden divine substance, the pneuma, the inner man, his soul, have fallen into the world, and these were imprisoned and are held captive by the demonic hosts of the demiurge. The very creation of man is a cosmic conspiracy against the hidden god of mercy. Man was created by the 'known god' to keep the pneuma, man's soul, sparks of the god of love, enchained, to prevent these divine sparks from reuniting with their source.

"The implications of this radical dualism, dear students of Torah, are self-evident. If the known, revealed world of experience and of history is the handiwork of an inferior creator, then every deed, every thought, every institution which affirms life and society, every act which would improve and perfect the terrestrial, the material and spiritual domain of the just god, places one in league with the demonic. Man's attempt to make things better only makes them infinitely worse. To live by the law, to do good —as understood within generally accepted civilized norms—is to be a tool of the demiurge. Matter is irredeemably evil; flesh and its desires, defiled; marriage, an obscenity; birth—maculate, polluted.

"Man's effort, these romantic mystics insist, bears the indelible stain of the demiurge's filth. For mortals of flesh and blood to participate effectively in their own redemption, they would have to skip over their own shadows—effectuate the most radical transvaluation of values—as futile an attempt as sitting on one's own lap or trying to jump out of one's skin. Only an act of grace on the part of the hidden god of love— vertical, apocalyptic, freely given, without a past; unrelated to the historic, horizontal strivings of humanity, independent of merit (over against it) will release man's soul from the bonds of the demiurge and his demonic legions. The true salvation of man and God is the end of the world—a cataclysmic destruction of the domain of the creator, when all the fallen sparks shall be liberated and ascend to reunite, in a blissful reconciliation, with their original source.

"Know, disciples of Torah," Rabbi Yonah urged, "that within this scheme of salvation—this soteriology—man and his actions count literally for naught. All that hopelessly trapped humanity can do is frustrate the designs of the demiurge, either by refusing to use the objects of his creation—an ascetic rejection of the things of this world; or by placing man above the laws of the 'just and vindictive' lawgiver—willfully violating, flouting, the ethical and moral precepts, the commandments of the creator god, in orgiastic debauch. The only worthwhile activity for man, his positive contribution to the salavation of his soul, is to arm himself with the hidden knowledge of the soul's way out of this world; to prepare himself for the hazardous ascent through the various spheres by mastering the secret names and formulas, the sacramental and magical rites which will immobilize the demonic agents who bar the way. The intricate, secret rituals and abracadabras defeat the hosts of the demiurge, the archons, who keep the soul imprisoned.

"There are endless subtleties, my colleagues, to these esoteric doctrines. The variations on the themes I have briefly and inadequately sketched for you exhaust the gamut of possibility. The expounders of these doctrines call themselves by many names; we lump them together, for convenience, under the general term Gnostics, 'the knowing ones,' the possessors and purveyors of the secret knowledge which is naturally hidden, unknowable—unattainable by discursive processes. Many of them are well versed in our Holy Scripture and excel in expounding its sacred texts to prove their heretical teachings.

"In the days of Rabbi Levi and Bar Kapparah, and for several centuries before them, these Gnostic doctrines were, in modified or extreme form, very widely disseminated. They influenced many of the central teachings of the Nazarenes. They even tempted some of our own great teachers. You recall that of the four masters who dared enter the 'orchard' of the esoteric and the arcane, only the giant Rabbi Akiba 'ascended and descended in peace.' Ben Azzai's fate was death. Ben Zoma, who beheld 'the eagle hovering over its nest both touching and not touching...' (cf. Deut. 32:11), went mad. And 'the other one' (Elisha ben Abuyah), the one 'who looked in ecstasy and cut down the shoots [became an apostate],' was doomed to permanent anonymity.

"The flirtation of a few of our great teachers, and of other small esoteric circles which still attract adherents, with aspects of gnosticism," Rabbi Yonah cautioned, "represents for us, sons of Torah, sobering incidents, valuable precedents to warn us of the hazards. Within Christianity, however, the adherents of a radical dualism, of a polarized universe of the god of law and justice over against the god of love and mercy, threatened to dominate the entire Church. The extremists among them, the followers of Marcion, ascribe our Torah—what the Nazarenes call the 'Old Testament'—to the tyrannous creator, and label us Jews, who uphold and teach 'the law,' as agents of the demiurge, the archenemies of the true god of love. They almost succeeded in establishing their doctrines as the orthodoxy of the Church. Only recently have they been placed outside the pale and their teachings branded as heresies by what is now the official religion of the Roman Empire. But many of the dualistic notions have, despite the official rejection, inextricably insinuated themselves into the central dogmas of Christianity and are daily used to vilify our Torah and our sacred commandments, our Creator and His beloved people.

"My colleagues, my teachers, whatever the source of these sectarian doctrines—be it pagan or Christian—we proclaim with our fathers, 'Not like these is the Portion of Jacob...' We have been assured through the prophet Isaiah:

"You are my witnesses," says the Lord, "...that you may know and believe me that I am He. Before me no god was formed nor shall there be any after me. I, I am the Lord and besides me there is no savior....I am the Lord, who made all things, who stretched out the heavens alone, who spread out the earth—Who was with me?—... I am the Lord and there is no other, besides me

*there is no God....I form light and create dark-
ness....I am the Lord who do all these things"
(Isa. 43:10 f.; 44: 24; 45:7).*

"In response to these very Gnostic teachings, as
expounded by a variety of pagan and Christian and
even some Jewish groups, our sages, centuries ago,
composed the two benedictions which we recite twice
each day before we proclaim the *Shema* and bear
witness to the onliness of God. Note the emphasis
in each phrase of these prayers. After we offer praise
to the Creator, the One who 'forms *light and darkness,*' who '*makes peace* and creates *everything,*' we
affirm: 'He who causes *light to shine in loving-kind-
ness* upon the earth and its inhabitants, renews daily,
in His *goodness,* the works of creation.' And in the
second blessing we continue, 'With an *eternal love*
have you *loved us....*you have taught our fathers the
laws of life....Our father, the Merciful One, have
mercy upon us and inspire us...to study, to teach, to
observe, to do and to establish all the words of your
Torah *in love....*Blessed are you, Lord, the One who
has chosen His people Israel *in love.*'

"With the rising and setting sun, we, the sons of

48

the eternal covenant, proclaim 'God is the only one.' And as we etch this central affirmation of our faith ever more deeply upon our minds and hearts, we prayerfully respond to those who would deny the core lesson of our historic experience. To those who seek the 'true god,' the god of love and light in the hidden and unknowable; to those who view the created world of human experience, both actual and potential, as an unrelieved curse; justice and law as the iron bars of this cave of shadows; to those who see salvation only in the destruction of the world, in a total rejection of and escape from it; to those who despair of mortal man, call his effort totally corrupt or, at best, irrelevant; to those who label us, sons of Torah, as the despised and rejected bearers of a covenant long since abrogated or even initially false and deceitful—to all of them we say:

Share our profoundest insight and our age-old commitment. Sing with us our daily love song to God and His creation. The lyrics were written by the Psalmist, the sweet singer of Israel (Psalm 19), "The heavens declare the glory of God and the firmament tells of His handiwork." (From creation to the Creator—the theme of the first

*blessing before the Shema in the daily liturgy—
the* Yotzer.*) And, "The law of the Lord (*torat
Adonai—*the 'tree of life') is perfect, restoring
the soul." (The Torah, revealed by God as an
act of love, bears witness to His essential nature
—the theme of the second benediction preced-
ing the* Shema, *the* Ahavah *blessing.)*

*Nature and history reflect the only God. Law
and love, justice and compassion are not contra-
dictories in mortal combat. They are aspects of
the One Creator. The tension between them is
the dialectical motive force, the breath of life in
the universe. Our vocation as the sons of the
covenant, binding till the end of history, is to
bear witness to His oneness, to perceive it as a
potential in creation and to make it actual in the
world of nature and men.*

"All that I have said, dear students of Torah,"
Rabbi Yonah explained, "the blessed Rabbi Levi derived from the form of the letter *Bet* in the opening
word of our sacred Scripture. Not an incidental
nicety, this lesson of Rabbi Levi's. He discerned a
central strand of the living Torah in one of the letters

of the Pentateuch. That is the genius of our Holy Testament—written and mostly oral: every minutest part, if probed deeply enough, implies all of it. The chain is present in each link; the wise and perceptive see the oak in every acorn.

"We give thanks unto God who has placed our portion among those who study and teach His Torah. Happy are we; how goodly our portion; how pleasant our destiny; how beautiful our heritage. Magnified and sanctified be His great Name, in this world which He created according to His will. May he cause His kingdom to reign speedily, in your lifetime and in the lifetime of all Israel..."

Rabbi Yonah concluded his discourse with the standard formula of praise, comfort, and consolation. Now, the other members of the academy, Rabbis and students, would add their contribution to the theme expounded by Rabbi Yonah.

IN THE ANCIENT ACADEMY

B. THE DISCUSSION

I.

After a brief recess, Rabbi Yonah called on one of his colleagues in the academy, the teacher of his son, the renowned Rabbi Yudan, to open the discussion. Because of his encyclopedic knowledge and almost total recall, Rabbi Yudan could be relied upon to cite numerous parallels from the tradition and to trace an interpretation of Scripture to its earliest source.

"The lesson derived by Rabbi Levi from the letter *Bet* of *Bereshit* and so lucidly expounded by the beloved head of our academy," Rabbi Yudan began, "was anticipated almost two centuries earlier by the sainted Aquila the Proselyte, the author of that most reliable and authoritative Greek translation of the Bible. In commenting on the first verse in Genesis, *Bereshit bara Elohim...*, he notes that, contrary to our expectation, the word 'God' *(Elohim)* appears only after the word for 'creation' *(bara)*—not *Elohim bara* but *bara Elohim*. Aquila concludes, therefore, that the good Lord places Himself after creation.

He would claim divinity, as it were, only after He creates. 'Unlike a mortal king who demands homage before achievement, before he has demonstrated his concern for his citizens, or contributed to their welfare, Aquila explained, 'the Holy One, blessed be He, creates first and only afterwards does He ask that we acknowledge Him as God. We become aware of Him, we address Him as God, not as a blind act of faith. We are led to Him by His creation —after experience and study and exposure. We discover Him in His creation.'

"Aquila's great contemporary, Shim'on ben Azzai, actually translated the first verse in Genesis as, 'First creation and afterwards God' *(Bereshit bara veaḥar kakh Elohim)*. He adds a deeper nuance to Aquila's exposition by interpreting the Genesis verse in the light of another biblical verse from the Book of Samuel. Ben Azzai understands David to say to God in his song of praise (2 Sam. 22:36) 'Your humility, (Lord,) has made me great.' God humbles Himself by giving primacy to creation. He exalts 'creature'; He gives dignity and worth to man by placing Himself after creation—as the final cause, the *telos* of creation. From creature to Creator—first creation and then God. God descends, so to speak, in order that man may ascend. He invests man, all creature, with ultimate purpose. They all testify and lead to Him.

"It is in this light," Rabbi Yudan continued, "that our forefathers, the tannaitic teachers, explained the fact that the Bible begins not with the Ten Commandments, the central imperatives, the heart of the Torah, but with creation and historical narratives. 'This is to be compared,' the Rabbis said, 'to one who entered a city and announced to the residents, "I would be king over you." The people replied, "Have you done anything for our benefit that you should reign over us?" So he proceeded to fortify the city, to improve their water supply, and he defended them against their enemies. When he subsequently said to them, "I would be king over you," the people responded with enthusiasm, "Yes! Yes!" Similarly, only after the Lord, in His mercy, redeemed Israel from Egypt, divided the sea for them, provided them with manna, a miraculous well, and defended them against the Amalekites—only after all these deeds did God say to Israel, "I would be king over you" ("I am the Lord your God who brought you out of the land of Egypt..."), and Israel replied, "Yes! Yes!"'"

"Nature and history, if probed deeply enough," Rabbi Yudan concluded, "elicit our affirmation of the King of kings. We come to know God, to recognize Him through the created world. We perceive Him in the rationality, order, oneness—both as an 'is' and as a 'could be'—in the constant flux and diversity of nature. When we behold beauty in the natural forms of the animate and inanimate world—we learn of God. We recite a blessing when we behold a tree in bloom, a beautiful or a wise human being. We discern God—we are commanded to bless —even in adversity, in the face of death. The stern demand of a father, the unconditioned love of a mother, the tender touch of a beloved, the innocent trust of a child—they all teach us the names of God. From infinite space to endless place; the wisdom of age and the ancient of days; the might of raging seas; the storm and the calm; the majesty of the mountain peak; the fear of being seen, of being judged; the torments of conscience; the nothingness of finitude; laughter and joy; man's striving, his reach for the immortal—they all reveal to us the faces of God. In the beginning was the deed—from creation to God. *Bereshit bara veahar kakh Elohim.*"

2.

Another of the senior members of the academy, Rabbi Yose, who shared the duties as head of the school with Rabbi Yonah, rose, after Rabbi Yudan concluded his remarks, to address the assembly of scholars and students. "To underline the centrality and significance of Rabbi Yonah's exposition," Rabbi Yose said, "I would share an incident told to me by my teachers. Though the event occurred two centuries ago, soon after the rebellion of Bar Kokhba against the Romans, it was considered of such crucial importance that a precise record of it was preserved and transmitted through the years. The central figure of the incident was Rabbi Natan the Babylonian, the second in authority in the academy at Usha, the close associate of Rabbi Meir, the older contemporary and teacher of Rabbi Judah Hanasi. And after these words of introduction, Rabbi Yose related the following tale:

A group of dualistic sectarians confronted Rabbi Natan in the presence of his colleagues and demanded to be heard. Despite his reluctance to enter into discussion with members of the numerous heretical sects which flourished in the second century, Rabbi Natan, impressed by the sincerity of the delegation and their obvious zeal, was persuaded to listen.

"You, Rabbi Natan, and most of your people," one of the delegation of Gnostics argued, "call the one and only God The 'Creator.' You claim that man discovers the names of the Lord, the attributes of the ultimate, in goodness and truth, through His creation—the world of experience. But please, dear Rabbi, look at this world, the handiwork of your God. Chaos, meaninglessness, senseless suffering and destruction, cruelty, hate, strife—unrelieved evil at every turn. Are these the faces of God? The senseless waste of nature—the sickly sweet smell of a million ants turning into dripping globs as we carelessly toss another log on the campfire; the moral indifference of the jungle, the murder of innocents, the crippling and death of children by hunger and disease and negligence—and worse yet, infants congenitally deformed; the suffering of the infirm and aged; war, pestilence, famine. Do these reveal the face of a god or of an unspeakably cruel monster?

"And you, you Jews, of all people—how can you, with your experience, persist in your piously naive affirmation? You have surely not forgotten—not so soon—the devastation of your land by the Romans, the rape of your women, the cries of your emaciated, starving children, the butchery of the finest and bravest warriors—all fighting for the glory of your Creator God! Is it not the vilest blasphemy to call the creator of these 'God'? Is not this very creation the most convincing proof that a vindictive, deceitful, capricious, tyrannical demiurge is the source and ruler of this world? God—the true, the good, the loving—is the unseen, the radically other, who stands over against this world, the eternal alien within it. He is to be found only by our attempting to transcend the pollution, the filth of creation."

Rabbi Natan would not enter into argument or engage in lengthy debate with the group of sectarians. He addressed them with deliberate calm. He gave testimony: "Many today, and no doubt throughout history, are irresistibly attracted by the morbid. They are overwhelmed by the absurd, the empty, the ugly—the monstrosities of existence. Everything shouts meaninglessness. Order, light, love are for them momentary incursions—shaded, strange, ill at ease, even delusory—into what they see as a vast wasteland. Reality, the normal, natural state as revealed by the past and present or by any conceivable curve that man may project into the future, is unmitigated darkness. The occasional glimmers of light and meaning are aberrations, temporary deviations from a dismal norm which inevitably reasserts itself.

"This view of nature and of human experience," Rabbi Natan continued, "appears especially cogent during periods of upheaval. The immediate impact of personal and communal tragedy, the widespread suffering and pain, color man's total perception. He is tempted to universalize the evil, to block out all light, to raise chaos to the level of ultimacy, and to hail the prince of darkness as the ruler—or, at the very least, the co-ruler—of the world. The essential element of this view is that chaos is invested with finality and ultimacy, or, in other words, that the shadows of existence are seen as aspects, as intimations and reflections, of a deity—even if he be but a deceitful god, a demiurge.

"We of the Congregation of Jacob have, from our very cradle as a people, chosen a very different perspective. The prophet Isaiah (45:18f.) summarized our view in a few pithy lines:

For thus says the Lord who created the heavens,
who formed the earth and made it... "I am the
Lord, there is no other. I did not speak in secret,
in a land of darkness. I did not say to the offspring of Jacob, 'Seek me in chaos.' I, the
Lord, speak the truth, I declare what is right."
Throughout our sojourn we have heard, and we
continue to hear, an insistent voice urging, de-
manding: Seek Me! Search the world to find Me!
Your vocation is to be the explorer; your destiny
—a continuous probing, an expedition of discovery. But your search will be futile if you seek
Me in chaos, in darkness. Not death but life; not
deceit but truth and right are the intimations of
my nature and presence. Do not dignify the
frightening shadows, the "not-yet," the primor-
dial slime not yet illumined by creative light,
by investing them with permanence and finality.
These are not where my glory dwells. You shall
glimpse the real insofar as you perceive the
"could me," the "shall be"—the permanent and
ultimate stuff of creation—in the transient and
ever-changing "is." You shall never see Me as I
am in my ultimate unity and perfection. I recede

as I am approached. As you arduously climb the mountain, your perspective changes; the range of your vision expands. Even if you reach the optimal vantage point—even if you scale the peak —you carry with you your finite world of "becoming"—an imperfect lens which distorts and reveals murky images. That is the inevitable limitation of your mortality. You perceive my presence in numerous guises. Man sees only refracted light; he calls Me by many names. Your quest must, therefore, continue till the end of time. But reflections of my presence do abound—tentative, problematic. The light often so dim and flickering that only men of acute vision—trained by millennial search—will perceive it; the voice so thin and small that it is audible only to those who have been conditioned to listen—by those who promised at Sinai, "We shall listen," and throughout their lives, twice each day, are reminded and exhorted, "Listen, O Israel..."

"Not easy! Not simple!" said Rabbi Yose at the conclusion of this tale. "Rabbi Natan's words mirror the difficulties, the anguish of his struggle. The path we have chosen bristles with obstacles. But the dangers of naivete, of a shallow optimism, are among the least of the hazards. Few, if any, are as intimately familiar with the bloodthirsty face of man, the scorching, pitiless desert sun, the parched winds, as we, the remmant of Israel. The ritual requirement that we read the Book of Lamentations and our martyrology is a formality. We need no reminders. The scars seared into our tenderest parts are reminders enough. No! Not a blind unawareness, not a rosy euphoria are our tempters. On the contrary, we have seen and experienced too much; we know too much; and too many of us cultivate an almost total recall. We would be less than human were we not to succumb, at times, and cry out in desperation with the same Isaiah, 'Truly you are a God who hides yourself...'

"How frightfully difficult not to be overwhelmed, shattered by the hammer blows of immediate, raw experience? How inhuman, heartless, 'As the infants and babes faint...in the streets of the city, as their life is poured out on their mothers' bosom' (Lam.

2:12), to urge encouragingly, 'Focus on the could-be; perceive the shall-be!' A hollow mockery! A colossal, cruel joke! How shall one with even a vestige of human compassion stifle the cry, 'You are a monster, God! Either you are a fiend or you do not exist. If you ever were, you are now impotent, dead. It is all a meaningless hoax!' And yet we persist. The anvil 'tempered in the furnace of pain' refuses to buckle. We adore 'the God of life, the king who delights in life.' Stubborn, stiffnecked—even Moses, our faithful shepherd, called us that—fanatic, foolhardy perhaps, but not naive.

"The insight of one who lives in sheltered innocence may superficially appear identical with the conclusion painfully reached after total exposure. But anyone who is aware of struggle knows that a wide gulf separates them; there is a qualitative disjunct between them. A commitment before knowledge and experience—the childlike, often childish innocence— vastly differs from the mature, resolute choice made after careful consideration of the options, after plumbing the depths. Paradise regained is not a cyclical repetition of paradise lost. The span of human history which begins 'east of Eden' works a radical transformation. The very fact of the Jew, his life and presence, must give pause. We who have seen and experienced, we who know, have the brazenness, the ḥutzpah, or is it a spark of divine courage and wisdom, to proclaim—not as an incidental nicety when the environment is receptive, but unto death—'He did not create the world a chaos. He made it to be inhabited...' Surely, such witness demands the most serious consideration. Perhaps more than the philosophers of negation and despair dream of is indeed possible. The history of the Jew, his lament and his song, are the depth of his perspective.

"The problems remain. They even become ever more complex. The original Adam was not the only one to spend the first night of his life in mourning for the sun—as tradition records—certain that it had set never to reappear. Most of us echo Adam's lament with each threatening cloud. At dusk, as darkness descends—an increasingly intense darkness, it seems —endless generations bewail the parting day, convinced that night has fallen forever. And before sunrise, where shall we find the evidence to prove them wrong? In the face of the chaos of day-to-day experience, we stand perplexed, shaken, our dreams a shambles. We scream our bitter disillusion, our pain, 'The innocent do suffer, the wicked prosper.' We curse and blaspheme. But somehow, as a formal ritual at first, and then—after we grope toward perspective—as the profoundest residue of our experience, we sing the song of our history. Not a logical argument is our song; not an abstract polemic or a facile solution. It is a stance, a gut response—a reach, a prayer. The variation is our own—the theme, as ancient as our collective memory. The song may now, because of our struggle, be more plaintive, in minor key perhaps; replete with discords, dissonances, disharmonies. But our version of the melody is deeper too, more honest—our reality:

The Rock, His work is perfect;
All His ways are just:
A faithful God, never false,
True and upright is He. (Deut. 32:4)

3.

Rabbi Yonah thanked his colleagues for their contributions. He was obviously pleased that they had found support for his exposition of the letter *Bet* of *Bereshit* in the exegesis of the great tannaitic teachers, Aquila the Proselyte, Shim'on ben Azzai, and Rabbi Natan, and even in the plain meaning, the *peshat,* of the Pentateuch and the Prophets. Rabbi Yonah underlined once more the importance of rooting one's thoughts in the tradition. "The Torah has been compared by our fathers," he recalled, "to a peg which secures and gives stability. Just as the tent stake makes firm and protects against capricious winds, so does the tradition.

"But remember too," he admonished, "that our Torah has also been called a 'young plant,' a tender shoot which grows and flourishes as a result of our devoted effort and care. The Torah urges that we magnify as well as glorify it—that we deepen, enlarge, and create Torah, that we cause it to grow." Turning now to the younger scholars and students, Rabbi Yonah encouraged them to share whatever thoughts his lecture and the discussion of his two colleagues had evoked in them.

The students, seated on the floor in semicircular rows, were evidently hesitant to express themselves in the presence of their teachers. But after an uneasy pause, one young student mustered the courage to rise and address the academy. "At the beginning of his discourse, Rabbi Yonah suggested that we ponder the various aspects of the first letter in our Torah, the *Bet* of *Bereshit*. And as our teacher probed the shape of the *Bet* and derived from it a central directive for our lives, the thought occurred to me that the numerical value of this letter, the number two, also teaches a similar lesson. I reasoned that the account of creation opens with the number two, the letter *Bet,* to teach us that the Merciful One created two worlds, this world and the world to come, the world of 'becoming' and the world of 'being,' the 'is' and the 'could be,' the real and the ideal.

"I found support for my conjecture," the student continued, "in a statement of Rabbi Yoḥanan as quoted by Rabbi Abahu: 'God created the two worlds, with the two letters of his name, *Y(a)H,* with the *Yod* and the *Heh*. This world was created with the incomplete letter *Heh* (ה), and the ideal world with the *Yod,* the letter written with a pointed stroke, a jot, on top of it (י), suggesting an ever-upward reach. The incomplete, the lack, the partiality of "becoming" (the incomplete letter *Heh*), along with the reach for, the vision of perfection, the ideal (the *Yod*), are implicit in the creative process. Man's experience of both aspects of creation, of the real and the ideal, leads him to the recognition of *Y(a)H* (ה י), to his discovering the name of God.'

"The numerical value of the letter *Bet,* the number two at the beginning of the creation story, implies the same lesson. The Torah tells us that creation consists of two worlds—the grasp and the reach—in constant interplay. The Creator, the one God, is manifest in an ongoing dialectical process in which the real is transformed by the ideal, while the ideal is continuously refined by the real. The creative movement induced by the opposition between the two worlds, the ever-moving point of tension, leads to the One —to the Source of all creation."

4.

Another young scholar, encouraged by the enthusiastic response to his colleague's effort, rose to offer his interpretation of the letter *Bet*. "The account of creation begins with a *B*, with the *Bet* of *Bereshit*," the student suggested, "because it is the letter of blessing; it is reminiscent of *Berakhah*, which also begins with a *Bet*. The first letter of the alphabet, the *Aleph*, recalls *Arirah*, 'curse.' Had the Lord opened the Torah with an *Aleph*, the heretics would surely have argued that our own Sacred Writ testifies to the corrupt nature of this world. 'Your Holy Bible,' they would have said, 'begins its account of creation with the letter of malediction, the *Aleph*. Can such a world, cursed at its core, survive?' Therefore did the Holy One, blessed be He, begin with the *Bet*, the letter of blessing, the *B* of *Berakhah*. At the very genesis our merciful Father informs us, 'Behold, I create the world with blessing; I implant a *Berakhah* into the heart of my handiwork. The fundamental bias of creation is beneficient; I intend it to be a benediction—a *Berakhah*.'

"The charge to our father, Abraham, 'You shall be a blessing,' *vehyeh berakhah* (Gen. 12:2), makes explicit what is implied in the *Bet* of *Bereshit*. The Holy One assigns the task of discovering, of actualizing, the blessing inherent as a potential in the universe, to Abraham and his seed. That is to be our vocation as the children of the patriarchs—to realize the *Bet,* the *Berakhah*—both the beginning and final goal of all creation. It is in this sense that we, the offspring of Abraham, are the instruments of an ongoing creative process. We entered into a covenant, we obligated ourselves; we chose the option available from the very beginning—to proclaim the *Bet,* to be a vehicle of blessing, so that through us 'all the families of the earth may be blessed' (Gen. 12:3)."

Rabbi Yonah rose from his seat after the student had concluded his remarks. The sage slowly descended into the audience. He embraced the youthful student and kissed him on his forehead. Rabbi Yonah turned to the assembly and said in a barely audible whisper—as if he were praying—"Dear people, had we come to hear only this final exposition, it would have been more than enough. Happy are we; blessed are we that such students of Torah are in our midst. We depart from the academy with gratitude in our hearts to our Father in heaven. With His unfailing help, we will find the blessing and make it known to all men."

V

IN THE CONTEMPORARY CLASSROOM

V

IN THE CONTEMPORARY CLASSROOM

The lesson completed, the teacher turns to address his students. "We read approximately six lines from our printed midrashic text. Despite the lengthy exposition, much has been left unsaid. We omitted all reference to the turbulent political currents in the middle of the fourth century—the unbelievable plots and counterplots, the power struggles of Constantine's successors, the machinations of Constantius in Rome and of Gallus at Antioch—the 'Christian' rulers of a crumbling Roman Empire. Julian the Apostate and his amazing effort to reverse the tide, with its profound implications for the Jews—his edict of toleration, and his attempt to rebuild the Temple in Jerusalem—are part of the scene, too. And so is the continuing controversy of the fanatical Athanasius—in and out of hiding and exile—with the followers of Arius. The early *Merkavah* mystics, the Manichaeans, the numerous and constantly changing

Christian 'heresies,' the endless subtleties in the interpretations of *Homoousion* or *Homoiousion*—whether 'the Father and the Son' were of identical or like or similar substance—and a myriad of cultural and social factors and day-to-day events, too insignificant to be recorded by historians but of overriding importance at the time, affecting the lives of thousands and the destinies of nations—all of these are part of the tool-world of Rabbi Yonah, Rabbi Yose, Rabbi Yudan, and their colleagues, and are reflected in their biblical 'exegesis.' All of these events are a part of the context of the halakhic and haggadic utterances of the Rabbis of the fourth century.

"But our lesson restricted itself to an analysis of the Jewish response to the challenge of gnosticism as reflected in the rabbinic dialogue with the first verse in Genesis. Our goal was to abstract, for the sake of clarity and effective communication, that which in Jewish experience never appears in isolation or as a theoretical abstraction, a single strand of the Jewish continuum—one component of the Jewish ethos."

* * *

Most of the students rush off with the first bell. A few young men are still at their desks, revising their notes or just staring out the window. The teacher, too, is still seated, the folio volume of Genesis Rabbah open in front of him. He is also reviewing the hour—attempting to assess the effectiveness of the session.

"The midrashic idiom, the form in which the Rabbis expressed their thoughts," he muses, "is a difficult obstacle for the contemporary student. The opening question of the rabbinic passage, 'Why does the Torah begin with the letter *Bet?*' undoubtedly alienated a number of them. Such minute probing of the biblical text may have served as an effective motivation for the Jew of antiquity. But in today's context this casuistic exegesis and its underlying assumptions are stumbling blocks; they intervene and discourage. The superior, tolerant smiles of a few of the members of the class clearly conveyed their dismissal of the rabbinic discussion as something quaint, remote—picayune. 'We know that *Bereshit*,' the bored stares complained, 'is a combination of a normal Hebrew prepositional prefix, the *Bet*, and *reshit*, a noun in construct form. Why disfigure a beautiful classic Hebrew sentence in order to use it as the handle for an idea alien to the original intent of the biblical author?'"

The teacher even sensed a subtle resentment, as if this rabbinic literature had let the students down. They would readily accept the remoteness of an Assyro-Babylonian or a Sumerian text and study it with a degree of enthusiasm and detached, intellectual interest. But this literary creativity of the Rabbis represents, they have been repeatedly told, 'living Judaism,' the source of their authority and, at some level, their very being as Jews. They ardently wished that this literature be edifying, exalted, heroic. The aspiring scholars' high expectations exacerbated their negative reaction—perhaps, overreaction—and intensified their disappointment. The instructor wondered what the reaction would have been had he chosen for his discussion one of the less exalted passages from rabbinic literature.

"But only a minority responded negatively," the teacher thought. "The majority of the class appeared interested; even fascinated by the range of ideas which the Rabbis derived from one letter in the Bible. They were impressed by the poetic imagination which could find a total orientation toward reality in the shape of a letter, or in its numerical value, or in the associations it evokes.

"But the interest of a number, even in this motivated group, was an impersonal one. They remained uninvolved. 'An interesting historical problem,' their attitude appeared to say, 'but not relevant for me, today. A Gnostic dualism, demiurge, an alien god—may have concerned the Jew of the early centuries of our era. But these are not our problems today. The myths are dead; the total framework remote, meaningless.

"'And the response of the Rabbis—that too, divest it of its subtle exegesis, the cute wordplay which give the impression of profundity; remove the symbols, the hazy images; strip the rabbinic formulation we analyzed today down to its essentials, and all that is left is a benign humanism, a naive meliorism—which Darwin, Marx, Nietzsche and Freud, the variety of neo-Malthusians and, perhaps most decisively, Auschwitz, have relegated to the limbo where all pious clichés dwell. If, after Babi Yar and Treblinka, an optimistic humanism in theistic or naturalistic form is still a viable option—and it obviously is for some—I much prefer the knowledgeable, sophisticated version of a Huxley or Teilhard de Chardin, a Fromm or Marcel or Buber...without the obfuscating midrashic rococo.'

"Such a reaction," the instructor comforted himself, "is not a total loss. The institutions and literature of Rabbinic Judaism have often made their most positive contribution in the opposition they aroused, as abrasives, when they evoked passionate rejection. The text we analyzed today is, of course, hardly one to elicit a violent negative response. But these students will be exposed to numerous other rabbinic texts—statements and passages which more obviously reflect dated, even gross and crass, time-place elements—regressive ethical notions, magic, and rank superstitions. These will convince the student of the impossibility of a fundamentalism, of attempting to find guidance and answers in the literal, in the specific details of an ancient literature which unavoidably expresses itself within the limitations of its milieu.

"But," the teacher mused, "the student's very rejection of the literal will lead him, if he persists and if his initial commitment is resolute, to find the true Torah—the Jewish continuum which transcends any limited, historical concretization of it. As important as the discovery and appropriation of the essential Jewish ethos undoubtedly is for a Jew, of no less significance—as an essential first step—is the knowledge, gained through firsthand probing of the endless details, that the specific, literal expression of the Jewish continuum in any one age may become, in a subsequent period, a gross disfigurement of it. Bibliolatry, the worship of the word, investing the human formulation with ultimacy, is perhaps the most persistent and pernicious form of idolatry; it stands in polar opposition to Torah. Failure to deny when deny we must is no less hazardous than failure to affirm when affirm we must. The living Torah is the result of the Jew's no as well as of his yes.

"Many Jews of the nineteenth and early twentieth centuries, the young intellectuals of the East European Pale, for example, embraced the humanism of the Russian intelligentsia, often with fanatic zeal. Their ardor would have been considerably less intense, too weak perhaps for the required sacrifice, had they not been reacting to the restraints of a talmudic Judaism which had degenerated into a fundamentalism and which controlled every minutia of their lives. The dammed-up energy held in check for centuries by a rigorously inhibiting tradition became, when finally released, a surging motive force. But it was also that tradition—in its deeper impulses, beyond the literal

—which directed that motive force to create modern Hebrew literature and a revitalized messianism—a vision of the imminent transformation of society to be realized through revolutionary socialism or through an activistic love of and return to the soil, the land of their fathers—to Zion. The positive role of tradition in their idealistic fervor was rarely given conscious recognition. It was most often denied. Only historical perspective reveals that it was very much present.

"It is not out of ignorance, nor is it a mere accident, that Tchernichowsky's Hebrew poem *Saḥ'ki,* with its refrain, 'I believe in man...,' written as a militant expression of a strident humanism, in defiance of religion, is today often sung with pious devotion in the synagogue. The Jew intuitively feels the profound religious theme in the poem, a depth rooting in Jewish tradition (the soulful melody to which the poem is sung is evidence of it), of which, within the limits of his situation, Tchernichowsky, himself, could not have been aware.

"A second-century Rabbi," the teacher did not resist his tendency to free associate, "saw this creative historic process of denial and affirmation, the no and yes, in the figure of a ripening pomegranate. As the pomegranate ripens, its skin dries and tightens and exerts ever-greater pressure on the seeds. The taut skin restrains and compresses and pushes inward, while the myriad of seeds, bursting with life, strain to escape. They thrust outward with the eagerness and enthusiasm of creation and birth. The dry, dead skin finally succumbs; it gives way under the pressure of life; it cracks—and the very force of its restraint now enters the seed to join it in its final creative thrust.

"The emergence of liberal forms of Judaism in the Western world followed a similar pattern. The reformers in Germany and the United States were impelled both by the restraining force of a stagnant tradition, still largely medieval in form, and by the attraction of the Enlightenment or the allure of the American dream, a 'frontier' messianism—concrete manifestations for them of the Jewish ethos when liberated from its Dark Age externals. What distinguished the American Jewish reformers was that, unlike the East European radicals, they consciously affirmed their rooting in historic Judaism; they saw their activity not as a break with their religious past— not as a disjunct—but as the true affirmation of it.

The age-old harvest—the overwhelming accumulation of a three-thousand-year Jewish experience—was turned over and over again, literally beaten, flailed, to liberate the kernels—the elements of the Jewish continuum. While they discarded the husk and the chaff, the pioneers of Reform Judaism cherished the precious seeds of grain. Due to the vastly different environment of the West—the Renaissance, the Reformation, the Industrial Revolution, the French and American Revolutions—the reformers of the United States, along with their predecessors in Germany, recognized and consciously identified their rejection of the time-place literal, of the dated and outworn, as an urgent Jewish imperative—as the demand of the highest reaches of historical Judaism. But their affirmation as well—their messianism, their universal concern, their vision of the Jew as a light unto the nations, as a blessing for all men—was the expression of their profound Jewish devotion, the here-and-now concretization of their Jewish ethos.

"Is it not the malaise of Reform Judaism today," the teacher reflected, "that for most of us tradition has ceased to function in either of its historic roles—either as a restraining or a motive force? We appear to have discarded the wheat with the chaff. Movement—vitality, dynamism—is the result of tension, a pull induced by the inhibiting reins of a past and the beckoning of an urgently desired goal, the attraction of an omega point, of a messianic vision of the future. We, liberal religionists, seem to have lost both sources of tension. Our messianism consists primarily of a genteel social meliorism, which, in most instances, lags somewhat behind the 'New Frontier' and the 'Great Society,' and, at the same time, we cavalierly dismiss the 'yoke of commandments'—the restraint of our moorings. All we seem to have left is the immediate present, and we are overwhelmed by it; we are floundering in it. We find ourselves in the dilemma of the adolescent struggling to constitute his own identity, whose nondirective, permissive parents deprived him both of a focus for his rebellion and of the positive elements he urgently requires for establishing his own ego integrity.

"One cannot, of course, artificially impose a religious discipline—not in a pluralistic secular society, and certainly not if the tradition is to serve primarily as a foil—as a focus for our rejection. But even if it were possible, we really do not want the accumulated overgrowth of this millenial heritage. Much, perhaps most, of the detail has long ago ceased to perform its protective or nourishing functions and is best discarded. Nor do we wish to recapture—except during rare moments of sentimentality and nostalgia—the crippling psychological effects, the syndrome of debilitating by-products, which inevitably result from an authoritarian religious discipline. We are well rid of all of that.

"But a serious confrontation, a struggle with the classic sources of our tradition out of a love, a respect, for our fathers and ultimately for ourselves—along with a regimen of Jewish rituals, symbols, and customs—will provide some of the deep roots of our historical heritage. The Jew who out of his own volition immerses himself in our traditional lore will be affected—at times, even transformed—by its spirit, even as he rejects, as he inevitably must reject, much of the literal content and most of the minute prescriptions."

The instructor was well aware, however, that these reactions—the ready dismissal after superficial exposure, and the somewhat more reluctant rejection as a result of deeper probing—were not those of the majority of his class. Most of the students were well beyond all of that. The exegetic form of the literature, the attempt of the Rabbis to root their thoughts in the Bible, underlined for these students the central importance of continuity in the experience of the Jew. They opened themselves to the poetry, the connotative depth of rabbinic metaphor and allegory. Many of them perceived and even experienced the reality behind the myth and symbol. They realized—more keenly than the others—that the biblical author of the first chapter of Genesis did not include in the *Bet* of *Bereshit* all that the Rabbis forced into that letter. But rather than their dismissing the midrashic method as a gross dishonesty, a wrenching out of context, they accepted the rabbinic procedure as the natural tool of the time, which reveals, if not the meaning of the Pentateuch, certainly, the mind and heart of the Jew. Rabbinic exegesis may not always illumine Bible—the book as written, the product of its own time. The commentary of the Rabbis is, however, the heart of Torah, of an ever-expanding "book" which absorbs within itself all that the Jew in each age hears as the word addresses him. These students grasped the essential nature of the Midrash

—that at its core, it is the record of the Jew's trans-forming Bible, a "book" (as the Greek etymology in-dicates), into Torah—into "here and now" events and imperatives. The midrashic method is of a piece with the anti-idolatry witness of the Jewish saga—the rejection of fundamentalism, of bibliolatry.

The challenges of a radical dualism, of the hereti-cal negation of the Creator, were more than distant historical aberrations for these members of the class. Behind the archaic symbolism, they perceived an ever-present reality—even some of the current head-lines. They saw the Gnostic phenomenon in its varied forms as a turbulent subterranean stream whose headwaters are hidden in the mists of prehistory and in the deepest layers of the human psyche. The many tributaries of this stygian flow surface from time to time and threaten to inundate the total landscape. The seductive, bittersweet melancholy of the roman-tic mood; the passionate mode with its unquencha-ble thirst, a ceaseless search for death in drama and art and religion...in politics; courtly love—the dark lust for the unattainable White Lady, La Belle Dame and Lorelei; the Albigensians; the flowering of the Kabbalah in the Provence and Spain in the twelfth and thirteenth centuries; back through the tortuous caverns to Mani and Valentius...and the Gospel according to John, and...Ahriman; surfacing again in aspects of Nietzsche, Freud's Thanatos,...the "eternal verticality" of the hipster—the *White Negro;* clearly on the surface in "Burn it down!" or the cynical, "What's the use; let's join them," or in the nihilistic drug cults; an enticing, sparkling brook in the lotus land of Eastern fads, the inviting stream to "no place," utopia...; a raging tide in splintering nationalism, napalm, the flame thrower, and the Bomb... and Auschwitz...; they are all variations of the same current coursing through ten thousand shadowed valleys.

And the rabbinic response? Creation! God of life! Blessing! The sensitive students heard the theme behind the variation. Not a philosophic argument this Midrash—but a vocation, a love song:

Be a blessing!
Open yourself to the possible!
Nurture an insatiable curiosity!
Find life-giving resource!

Not a specific directive for each situation; not a literal blueprint to be automatically applied—and surely not a withdrawal from the inevitable pain and mystery of human experience. But whatever the price—in extremis—uncover the blessing, find the *Bet;* as shallow or as profound as the life of a people who refuse to die; yet have risked death a thousand times to affirm life and the God who desires life—*Melekh Ḥafetz Baḥayyim.*

VI

THE SOURCES

VI

THE SOURCES

In my reconstruction of Rabbi Yonah's lecture and the responses of his colleagues and students, I draw upon much of the entire literature. The language is contemporary, and in some instances, no doubt, I go beyond the original intent of the text and its authors. I believe, however, that I have remained faithful to the essential spirit of the literature. The rabbinic response to the Gnostics of the first or second or fourth centuries is of significant relevance as we confront the forms of gnosticism much in evidence in our own day. The basic challenge in the second century, when freed of the changing mythologies, shares much with the mood today. And the response of the Jew in the early centuries of our era is an alternative, an option which a searching, thinking human being would do well to confront seriously as he struggles to formulate his program of existence and his basic stance in life.

Though I obviously cannot reproduce the entire

apperceptive mass implicit in my analysis of the rabbinic argument, I cite the texts which served as my basic points of departure.

A.

The following are the texts, in literal translation, on which I based Rabbi Yonah's exposition (Chapter IV-A).

1.

"In the beginning God created..." (Gen. 1:1). Rabbi Yonah said in the name of Rabbi Levi, "Why was the world created with the letter *Bet*? Just as the *Bet* is closed on its sides and open only in front, so may you not search what is above, what is below, what is before and what is after."

Bar Kappara said, "The biblical verse, 'You have but to inquire about bygone ages that were before [*l'faneikha*, 'in front of'] you, *since the day that God created...*' (Deut. 4:32), means that you may only investigate the time since the creation of days, but you may not search that which preceded it. Probe only 'from one end of heaven to the other,' the verse continues (ibid.), but you may not probe beyond it."

—Genesis Rabbah I.10 (Ed. Theodor, p. 8).

The passage (with some significant variants) occurs in the Jer. Talmud, Ḥagigah II.1, 77c, and in the Pesikta Rabbati XXI (ed. Friedmann, p. 108b). For the full implications of this passage, the following classic sources should be studied: Mishnah Ḥagigah II.1; Tosephta, Ḥagigah II.1 and 7; Jer. Talmud, Ḥagigah II.1, 77a and 77c; Babylonian Talmud, Ḥagigah 11a and 14b.

2.

Rabbi Lazar, the son of Avinah, in the name of Rabbi Aḥa said, "For twenty-six generations the letter *Aleph* complained before God. It said in His presence, 'Master of the universe, I am the first of the letters; why did you not create your world with me?' God said to it, 'The world and its fullness was created only in the merit of the Torah. On the morrow, when I will give my Torah at Sinai, I will begin only with you, 'I am the Lord your God...' [*Anokhi Adonai Elo-heikha*]" (Exod. 20:2).

—Genesis Rabbah I.10 (Ed. Theodor, p. 9).

Note the parallels cited by Theodor in his commentary, *Minḥat Yehudah.*

3.

Four entered the orchard [*Pardes*], Ben Azai, Ben Zoma, Aḥer [the "other one," Elisha b. Abuyah], and Rabbi Akiba. One gazed in ecstasy and died; one gazed in ecstasy and went mad; one gazed in ecstasy and cut down the shoots; and one ascended in peace and descended in peace.

Ben Azai gazed in ecstasy and died. Concerning him Scripture says, "Precious in the sight of the Lord is the death of his saints" (Ps. 116:15). Ben Zoma gazed in ecstasy and he went mad. Concerning him Scripture says, "If you have found honey, eat only enough for you, lest you be sated with it and vomit it" (Prov. 25:16). Elisha gazed in ecstasy and cut down the shoots. Concerning him Scripture says, "Let not your mouth lead you into sin..." (Eccles. 5:5). R. Akiba ascended in peace and descended in peace. Concerning him Scripture says, "Draw me nigh, we will run after you; (the king has brought me into his chambers)..." (Song of Songs 1:4).

—Tosefta, Ḥagigah II.3–4.
Cf. Jer. Ḥagigah II.1, p. 77a;
Bab. Ḥagigah 14 b.

4.

Rabbi Yehoshua was walking on the highway and Ben Zoma was coming toward him. When he reached him, Ben Zoma did not greet him. Rabbi Yehoshua said to him, "Where from and where to, Ben Zoma?" He said to him, "I have been peering intently at the Work of Creation [ma'aseh bereshit] and not even a handbreadth separates the upper and lower waters, as it is written, 'and the spirit of God hovered over the face of the waters' (Gen. 1:2). Scripture also states, 'Like the eagle that stirs up its nest (that flutters over its young)...' (Deut. 32:11). Just as this eagle hovers over its nest both touching and not touching, thus, not even a handbreadth separates the upper and lower waters." Rabbi Yehoshua said to his disciples, "Ben Zoma is already on the outside." Not many days passed and Ben Zoma died.

—Tosefta, Ḥagigah II.6.

This passage, with significant variants, also appears in: Jer. Ḥagigah II.1, 77a; Bab. Ḥagigah 15a; Genesis Rab. II.4, p. 17.

5.

R. Yudan said, "Scripture concludes the account of the creation on the first day with the phrase, 'and it was evening and it was morning, one day' (Gen. 1:5) [using the cardinal "one" instead of the expected ordinal, "first"] to teach that on that day God was alone, the only one in the world."

R. Lulinei, the son of Tabrei, in the name of Rabbi Yitzḥak said, "...All agree that no being was created on the first day, in order that you shall not say that Michael stretched the firmament in the south, Gabriel in the north, and the Holy One, blessed be He, pulled in the middle, but 'I am the Lord, who made all things, who stretched out the heavens alone, who spread out the earth, *me-iti*' (Isa. 44:24). Though tradition vocalizes the last word in the verse, *me-iti*—'from Me,' it is written *mi-iti* [the *ketiv*]: 'Who was with Me? Who was a partner with Me in the creation of the world?'"

—Genesis Rabbah III.8, p. 24.
Cf. Gen. Rab. I.3, p. 5, and
parallels noted by Theodor.

B.

The following are the texts, in literal translation, on which I based Rabbi Yudan's response (Chapter IV-B).

I.

Rabbi Yudan, in the name of Aquila, commented on the biblical verse, "In the beginning God created..." (Gen. 1:1) [noting that *bara* precedes *Elohim*]: "It is appropriate to address this One (the Creator), 'God.' A king of flesh and blood exalts himself in a province before he has built public baths for the inhabitants, before he provides for them canals, dykes."

Shim'on ben Azai said, "This is what David meant when he exclaimed, 'Your humility (Lord) has made me great' (2 Sam. 22:36). A mortal mentions his name before his achievements (title, praise)—so-and-so augustali (his title of honor), so-and-so followed by his title. But the Holy One, blessed be He, is not so; only after He provides for the needs of his world (only after *bara*), does He mention his name: 'In the begining He created,' and only afterwards, 'God.'"

—Genesis Rabbah I.12, pp. 10 f.
Cf. parallels cited by Theodor.

2.

"I am the Lord, your God…" (Exod. 20:2). Why were the Ten Commandments not spoken at the beginning of the Torah? They cited a parable as an illustration: This matter is to be compared to one who entered a province and said to them [the inhabitants], "I would be king over you." They said to him, "Have you done anything of

benefit for us that you should reign over us?"
What did he do? He built for them the fortified
wall; he brought water for them; fought wars
for them. He said to them, "I would be king over
you." They said to him, "Yes! Yes!"

Thus, the One called Place [*Ha-Makom*]
brought Israel forth from Egypt; He split the sea
for them; He caused manna to descend for them;
He brought up for them the (miraculous) well;
He drove up the quail for them; He waged the
battle of Amalek for them. He said to them, "I
would reign over you." They replied to him,
"Yes! Yes!"

—Mekhilta Baḥodesh, Yitro V
(Ed. Horovitz, p. 219).

C.

I based the discussion of Rabbi Natan with the Gnostics (Chapter IV-B-2) on the following Midrash:

"I am the Lord your God (who brought you out
of the land of Egypt)..." (Exod. 20.2). Why was
this said? Because He was revealed at the sea as
a brave warrior, as it is said in Scripture, "The

103

Lord, the Warrior..." (Exod. 15:3); He was revealed at Sinai as an old man full of loving mercy, as it is said in Scripture, "And they saw the God of Israel: (under his feet there was a likeness of a pavement [*livnat*] of sapphire)"; and when they were redeemed, what does it say? "Like the very sky for purity" (Exod. 24:10); Scripture also says, "A I looked, thrones were placed (and one that was ancient of days took his seat...),", and it says, "A stream of fire issued and came forth from before him...(the court sat in judgment and the books were opened)" (Dan. 7:9–10); in order not to provide an opportunity for the nations of the world to say, "There are two powers (deities)"; but, "I am the Lord your God..." (Exod. 20:2), I am the one in Egypt and I am the same one at Sinai; I am the one of the past and I am the one of the future; I am the one in this world and I am the one in the world to come"; as it is said in Scripture, "See now that I, I am He (there is no God beside Me...)" (Deut. 32:39); and it says, "Even unto old age, I am He..." (Isa. 46:4); and it says, "Thus says the Lord, the King of Israel and his

Redeemer, the Lord of hosts; 'I am the first and I am the last; (besides Me there is no god)'" (Isa. 46:6); and it says, "Who has performed and done this, calling the generations from the beginning? I, the Lord, the first and with the last; I am He" (Isa. 41:4).

Rabbi Natan says, "From here we deduce a refutation of the sectarians [*minim*] who say that there are two powers. For when the Lord arose and said, 'I am the Lord, your God,' who stood up to challenge him? If you were to argue that the matter occurred in secret, has it not already been said in Scripture, 'I did not speak in secret (in a land of darkness…)'; (and if you were to argue that) I give it only to these; 'I did not say to the offspring of Jacob, "Seek me in chaos (Isa. 45:19)."' Nor did I give it as a deceiver. Scripture says thus, 'I, the Lord, speak the truth; I declare what is right' (Isa. 45:19)."

—Mekhilta, Baḥodesh, Yitro V (Ed. Horovitz, pp. 219 f.; cf. p. 206).

Cf. also Ed. Lauterbach, vol. 2, p. 232 and variants.

D.

The response of the first student (Chapter IV-B-3) is based on the following rabbinic texts, in literal translation:

1.

Another explanation: Why was the world created with a *Bet*? In order to let you know that there are two worlds. [The numerical value of the letter *Bet*.]

—Genesis Rabbah I.10, p. 9

2.

Rabbi Abahu, in the name of Rabbi Yoḥanan, said, "The two worlds, this world and the world to come, were created with two letters, one with the letter *Heh* and one with the letter *Yod*. What is the scriptural proof? '...*ki beyah Adonai ẓur olamim*' (Isa. 26:4). [The Rabbis translate this verse: 'With Y[a]H, the letters *Yod* and *Heh,* the Lord fashioned the worlds.'] We still do not know which one of them was created with the *Yod*. It is, however, clarified by the scriptural verse (Gen. 2:4), 'These are the generations of the heavens and the earth when they were created [*behibaram*].' Read not *behibaram,* but *be-Heh baram.*) He created them with a *Heh* and the world to come with a *Yod...*"

—Yer. Ḥagigah II.1, 77c.
Cf. b. Menaḥot 29b;
Gen. Rab. XII.10, p.
109; and the many parallels cited by Theodor.

E.

The response of the second student (Chapter IV-B-4) is based on the following rabbinic text:

Another explanation: Why was the world created with a *Bet*? Because it is the language of blessing [*Berakha*]. And why not with an *Aleph*? Because it is the language of curse [*Arirah*].

Another explanation: Why not with an *Aleph*? In order not to provide an opportunity for the sectarians [*minim*] to say, "How can the world endure when it was created with the language of curse?" But the Holy One, blessed be He, said, "Behold I create it with the language of blessing, would that it endure."

—Genesis Rabbah I:10, p. 9.

Typography and Design by Noel Martin

תורה בצו
תמוש 1875 למ
=
1975
יבקר אור